The Rose Trilogy

Three short stories by
Maria Tedeschi

2022

Prima edizione: settembre 2022

2022 Maria Tedeschi
ISBN: 9798353748946 (Independently published)
Proprietà letteraria e artistica riservata
Original title: La Trilogia delle Rose by Maria Tedeschi
Bookdesign: Keyprint SA
Cover : Sonja Taggiasco
Special thanks to *Amanda Blee.*

This collection is a work of fiction. Names, characters, businesses, events and incidents are the products of the author's imagination. Any resemblance to actual persons, living or dead, or actual events, is purely coincidental.

For Anna, who smelled of roses and loved coffee. Who aged with grace and beauty, and had the innate ability to renew herself, while staying true to her nature, thanks to the power of prayer and a smile.

Introduction

When it comes to short stories, Maria Tedeschi's Rose Trilogy is unique in its originality and expressive vivacity.

It presents the theme of "talking objects", reminiscent of early Latin literature, in a new key.

As Signora Rosa's coffee pot tells its story, intertwined with the external and interior life of its owner, it gradually takes on a new dimension of "humanity", we see it transform from a simple object into a sentient being, endowed with sensitivity, emotions, memories and moods.

In this trilogy, each thing, each event, each person, each part of the narrative, is brought to life, crystalising in the memory, in an impalpable space-time moment that evokes an inner journey, marked by fleeting but undying moments, which the writer relives and shares with her readers.

It is synonymous with the profound search of the self, in the most authentic, most liberal sense of the word, a sensory experience that unmasks the character, or characters who, as Pirandello would have said, were created, more or less consciously, by fear or convenience during the course of their existence. The empathic reader is drawn in, word after word, line after line, in the vertigo of its most visceral need for liberation from the stereotypes in which they are encapsulated, from the constraints of a life lacking in authenticity. However, not before they find themselves overwhelmed by the inner turmoil that, since childhood, represents the sublime charm of the unzconscious, finally finding the courage to "be".

Miss. Annalaura Confuorto
(Doctor of Law)

Author's Note

Why a trilogy?

The number Three, so powerful and full of meaning, has always fascinated me.

Three is the synthesis of the even (two) and the odd (one), the symbol of the Christian Trinity and the exit from antagonism. It overcomes the partial, reductive, and contrasting vision of dualism between two opposing realities: right/wrong, beautiful/ugly, innocent/guilty, man/woman.

Three is also the symbol of the trifurcation of the plant when its branches sprout. Almost as if in the number Three, thoughts multiply and expand, becoming simultaneously mother, father, and son, and therefore breathing life into our future.

The Kabbalah associates the number Three with Ghimel (ג), the third letter of the Hebrew alphabet. The figure of

Ghimel (ג) reminds me of a runner, one foot pushing forwards as if trying to escape their own limitations, from a paralysing, immobilising stasis.

The figure of Ghimel:

ג

In the *Smorfia*, the book which details the old Neapolitan tradition of analysing dreams and converting them into Lotto numbers, the number Three is synonymous with *'a jatta* (the cat): an animal known for always landing on its feet, its strong natural instinct, and the way it faces every situation, even the worst, in almost total autonomy.

Why roses?

Every rose, through its extraordinary variety of scents and vibrant colours, conveys a message, often quite contrasting in meaning.

The rose is both good and evil - loved by witches and fairies alike. Often associated with ethereal beauty, but also with pain and deception, due to the dangerous thorns along its stem. Its constant flowering and fading is a cyclic perpetuation towards other dimensions of 'being', it is in a continuous phase of 'becoming'. Its fragrance can give excellent psychological and physical support and ease inner conflicts, helping us find peace and serenity within moments.

The Yellow Rose is the happiest colour. It is a symbol of vivacity but also of jealousy. It stimulates and boost self-esteem in moments of despair.

The Red Rose represents feelings, like passion and extreme love, powerful and, sometimes, imperfect feelings. That isn't all that it represents, however, it has other, secondary meanings.

Finally, the pink rose symbolises affection and friendship. It conveys a message of affinity, friendship and loyalty, the absence of malice and ulterior motives, simplicity, light-heartedness, and admiration, but also the existence of a recent, innocent love.

For these stories, I took inspiration from my studies of

Japanese literature, in particular, the philosophy of Wabi Sabi and the way it captures beauty in imperfection, appreciating simplicity and accepting the transient nature of everything.

As an alternative to the way we face the challenges of modern life and its limitations, it suggests we simply slow down and simplify the complications of our day to day life by focusing on what really matters: our passions, our dreams, which are often left by the wayside when we're "sadly" realistic. We're surrounded by a myriad of possibilities but we fail to see them because they lie just beyond our fears of possible failure. Those fears will always exist, but their purpose should be to strengthen our capacity for resilience. The beauty of sincere simplicity can be found in the inexorable passage of time, the serene understanding of nostalgia and the imperfection of a sweeter, deeper tension.

Maria Tedeschi

The work is published in self-publishing and the author holds all rights of the same in an exclusive manner. No part of it may be reproduced without her prior consent.

The Yellow Rose

Image courtesy of the Italian Cultural Institute of Paris.

The Yellow Rose

It's said that in the garden of a famous Parisian institute, there grows a very rare yellow rose. On warm May nights, it exudes a scent of coffee that mingles with the delicacy of the damask roses: in an intense and captivating scent that tells of love and life.

I am a Neapolitan coffee pot, a mocha, a descendant of the noble family of the *cuccumelle*, and our art is the production of the king of coffees.

Coffee, that magical juice with extraordinary powers. In its lineage it boasts the genes of ancient Ethiopia, of the Arabian Peninsula and many more. Originally known as *K'hawah*, which means "refreshing", it brings joy, strength, solidarity, friendship, and beauty, dispelling negative thoughts and fatigue. A social drink, it accompanies any kind of relationship, is perfect in any circumstance and is never intrusive.

Just a few days ago, I celebrated my tenth birthday. Immediately after, my owner's heirs, taking advantage of her recent passing, and while I was still full of coffee, instead of throwing me a party, threw me unceremoniously into the rubbish. As the great Totò would have said, "Gentlemen are born, and they were not born gentlemen!"

I wasn't expecting a gold statue, just a little gratitude for my years of service: I'd made them happy, encouraged them, comforted them, helped them stay awake, supported them through the hard times...but no - as thanks, I was replaced by a state of the art coffee machine! Proof that they prefer a heartless robot with no imagination, where the pod is god: whether it's barley coffee, ginseng, decaf, etc, it's all mass produced and soulless.

So, there I lay, surrounded by what *Signora* Rosa's heirs considered "useless junk", unwanted, devoid of value. She'd only just been laid to rest and they were already permanently erasing any memories of her. Why didn't they throw out her ruby brooch or her diamond earrings too? They were much older than me and showing their age. Why did they have emotional value and I didn't?

Donna Rosa only wore them on special occasions, I kept her company all day, every day. When it was hot and the window was open, my aroma would seep through the alleyways, filling them with my goodness or, in winter, when the window remained closed, my precious scent filtered through the rooms, tickling the nostrils of those present. I was always there, supporting her through her troubles, the tears, the laughter. Always. And where were they? Locked away in a box, only making themselves useful on stupid, formal occasions. And the reward for my loyalty was being tossed out into the cold, in a metal box, full of an anonymous pile of stinking refuse. They didn't even empty me! I'm still half full! I don't need a rest, I'm too young to retire, I can still work. I've got so much left to give, please don't leave me here. I don't like the cold and I hate being alone!

"Oh, shut up! You're not the only one who got thrown out without a word of thanks," cried a bundle of yellowing papers from a pile of old cardboard and scrap paper.

"Who are you? And what makes you think you were as close to Donna Rosa as me?"

"I'm her notebook, the one where she kept her accounts, where she wrote her shopping lists, her thoughts, and the numbers from the *Smorfia*. Those heirs of hers didn't even have the curiosity to open me. They have no idea how many of them I have inside me, how many memories I have here on these old pages. They just threw me out without a second thought. It's all here; when Giada got her first tooth, her childhood illnesses, what little Terenzio would and wouldn't eat, all the special moments - then there's her husband, Rubicondo and his obsession with those buxom women he called *'e piezz' 'de carne*... It's all here, her pain, her friends' secrets, and much more."

"Grr! Don't talk to me about those heartless people," replied the coffee pot. "I don't want to know anything about them, so please don't mention them again. If you really want to read me something, let me hear something about my mistress. And I don't mean her accounts or her recipes either, I've heard them all before. What I really want to know is, did she ever mention me?"

"Let me see... okay... it's from a long time ago, but... Thought Number Forty-Two, *'o ccafè*. It says, Bought a new coffee pot today. The latest model, a little more than I wanted to pay, but good quality, it'll come in very handy."

"Is that all?"

"Unfortunately, yes, but if you have something to add, go ahead, that way we can get to know each other, and take our minds off the cold and the stench of the organic waste. Did they really have to dump it right here?"

"Okay, I'll start, then you can read me some more of her thoughts...It all began when Donna Rosa saw me in one of those bargain stores, just down the road. I was there, on the shelf, next to a display of China plates and crystal glasses, the ones that usually cost and arm and a leg. I was the latest model, strong and resistant, fresh off Mr. Bialetti's production line. Everyone loved me, everyone wanted me, but they were put off by my price. 15,000 lire was a lot in those days, it was a real investment.

"As soon as *Signora* Rosa saw me, her eyes lit up. It was love at first sight. She couldn't resist me. She rummaged in her purse, counting her cash. She even put off getting her hair permed at Gelsomina's so she could afford me.

"I promised excellent service, guaranteeing that I was perfect for her: a brand new, two-cup Moka, durable and high-quality, was just what she needed for a busy home like hers with lots of visitors, where they drank coffee, day and night. And that's how I became part of the family. They trusted me. My coffee was always there, a ritual for every occasion, for whispered secrets, sickness and celebration, over business discussions - whatever the occasion, I was there, even consoling them in moments of loss and grief.

"And I worked hard, too. Just from the way she filled me, I knew whether the guest was welcome or not, whether they were part of the family or an outsider. For close relatives, *Signora* Rosa, would fill my filter until it was overflowing.

However, if it was for a stranger or someone she didn't like, she left the filter practically empty, so I produced *'nu cafè lasco*, as weak and watery as the relationship between my mistress and whoever was visiting.

"Oh, how I loved her though! We had the same taste, we understood each other, and immediately became best friends. The way I prepared coffee was the perfect expression of our feelings. Like I said, I was always hard at work. Pretty soon I knew all the secrets of the family and its friends, their moods, their hopes, disappointments and difficulties, until I became an expert in matters of the human soul. Discreetly, my coffee brought relief, it accompanied, prepared, lifted the spirit and, when necessary, helped overcome even the most difficult moments – and, let me tell you, in those ten years, there were many!

"When Donna Rosa had her closest friends over, like *Signora* Venezia (a vulgar, working class woman who, despite having little in common with my mistress, had a genuine friendship with her), she'd serve strong black coffee, adding the sugar directly to my top chamber, and serving it in double cups without saucers, on a small tray - a sign of great friendship.

"Extra strong coffee improves relationships, loosens the tongue and makes it easier to confess secrets and confidences. *Signora* Venezia only spoke dialect, but my mistress never made her feel uncomfortable. She listened to her problems, gave her advice and often smoked a cigarette with her in secret.

"Venezia had married young. She had four daughters to marry off and her husband was the only one working. Knowing money was tight, Donna Rosa always set a little food aside for her and Venezia paid her back with the odd job around the house, ironing her husband's trousers, or simply bringing her freshly picked flowers from the country. My mistress was always so good and kind, and her generosity wasn't just financial, it went far beyond the material side of things. She was a true Lady and, as we know, Ladies are born, not made.

"With people she didn't consider family, or she didn't like very much, however, she'd make the coffee as weak as possible. She'd pour it into cups with matching saucers, all served on an old-style Sheffield silver tray, one of those with handles, together with teaspoons and a sugar bowl. It was just swill, as weak as her feelings for the people she made it for, like *Signora* Valestra or *Signora* Rasa, as common as muck, who rented land from my mistress. I heard they made their money on dodgy deals, which was very likely, they always looked so shifty! They often came to see Donna Rosa. Always empty handed and always the same excuse, they'd been passing and decided to drop in on the off chance. Before they left, however, they always managed to scrounge free tax advice from Donna Rosa's husband, *Commendatore* Rubicondo, a very respected accountant.

"There's nothing worse than a *'perocchie sagliute m'perteca,* a presumptuous person,' my mistress used to say, 'so why waste time and energy on them?'"

The Yellow Rose

"Both 'ladies' were regulars in the *Commendatore's* study and he was very favourable towards them. In fact, he seemed to appreciate their visits, and their curves, very much. To me, they looked like two balls of lard in too tight clothing, sometimes even two sizes too small. They were so tightly squeezed into their clothes, which seemed to get tighter and tighter, that they looked like balloons, ready to burst at any minute. No wonder my mistress used to call them *Les Madames Boules de Suif*: the Dumplings.

"In the mornings, I'd make sure the mistress started the day with a nice strong coffee, to give her energy and put her in a good mood, and she'd look at me the same way she looked at her family, with love and admiration. She always did, even when the doctor, that genius at the hospital, stopped her from drinking coffee. Suddenly it was bad for her. She wasn't bothered, though. Every morning she'd fill me up, then pour herself a cup of coffee, breathe in the perfume, then pour it over her beloved yellow roses, which grew more beautiful and luxuriant by the day. When her time came, her last wish was *'na tazzulella 'e cafè*, a cup of coffee, and I'm proud to say that she died with me in her mouth. So, dear Notebook, now you know about me, tell me about yourself."

"I'm just a notebook. I belonged to Giada, Donna Rosa's oldest daughter, she hadn't used me in years. When the mistress found me, instead of throwing me away, she turned me upside down and gave me a new life. I was everything to her: she'd write down what bills needed paying, recipes she heard on the radio, telephone numbers and, every now and then, she'd write down her thoughts, then look up their meanings and numbers in the *Smorfia*.

"I may have been just an old notebook, but I was always with her and she always respected me, like she did everyone else. She made me feel real, like a person. Whatever it was, there was some emotional bond that united us. I'll read you some of her thoughts...

"Number 79: *'o mariuolo* (The Thief) - Donna Rosa wrote, 'At the cemetery this morning, I saw a gypsy steal one of my yellow roses from *Maresciallo* Baffuto's grave. He didn't know I'd been watching him. At first I was going to shout at him, but then I offered to buy it off him. For that skinny little man, my rose smelled like a loaf of bread, but for the *Maresciallo* it was a mere decoration. When he was gone, I put it back on the *Maresciallo's* grave and he seemed to be smiling, so perhaps he could smell it after all.

"Number Thirty-five: *l'aucelluzz* (The Bird) - Today I found a little sparrow on the balcony. It was so weak, it couldn't even stand. It wasn't scared, it let me get up close, so I gave it some breadcrumbs soaked in water and walked away. Birds and angels have a lot in common, you can tell by the wings, and sometimes they come to visit, bringing spiritual messages.

"Numbers Twenty-one: *'a femmena annura* (The Naked Woman) and Seventy-one: *l'omme 'e mmerda* (The Scoundrel) - Sometimes we meet people who, because of their attitude, something they say or do, we immediately consider obnoxious. You want to avoid them like the plague, but you can't help bumping into them. Even worse, sometimes you come home to find them in the house...

"5th January, *Signora* Rasa came to visit today. She just happened to choose a day when I'd usually be at Gelsomina's getting my hair done. Two other women were with her. Gelsomina wasn't open today, though. Her son fell downstairs and banged his head so she had to take him to hospital. So I came home. Just as I opened the door, I heard cheerful music and low voices coming from my husband's study. Thinking he was preparing a surprise for me, I crept over and peeped inside. What I saw was *Signora* Rasa in her underwear.

"Her backside was like a huge balloon and her bosoms hung down like two saddlebags full of old, mushy melons, the ones my gardener feeds the pigs. Two other women were busy cavorting half-naked around my husband while he, grinning like an idiot, slipped 10,000 lire notes in their knickers. When they saw me, they tried to pull down their cheap dresses, which were up around their necks. I got the broom and chased those floozies out the door, and all the time my husband was making useless excuses. I didn't listen to him, obviously, I just pretended. He's gone too far this time, I don't think I can ever forgive him. That's what happens when you only think of yourself, and forget how much your behaviour can hurt other people.

"I lost all trust in him, he's a stranger to me now. It was like a bullet to the heart and I think that was when I started to get sick.

"Number Twenty-seven: *'o càntero* (The Chamber Pot) - Anything that is locked up, either stinks or rots, like an old chamber pot. My husband's wardrobe has the same smell. It reminds me of the past and dark times. I've decided to open the door and windows and let some fresh air in. I have to do the same to my mind too, if I don't want it to start rotting. There's an unbearable stench of bodies and chamber pots!

"Number Seventeen: *'a disgrazia* (Misfortune) - I haven't been able to write anything, or even think, for months. Nothing fits me anymore. I've lost weight and I'm as weak as a kitten. My consultant said he doesn't know if it will help, but I have to eat lots of vegetables and drink plenty of orange juice. I try to do everything he says, but I see no improvement. My head aches all the time, my whole body hurts, and every day I get weaker and weaker. It feels like I'm becoming invisible.

"Today *Signora* Venezia came to see me. She cried all the time, sobbing, 'It's such a shame!' I've been thinking and I know I don't have much time left. The pain doesn't bother me, I've already come to terms with it, so I'm going to embrace the uncertainty and choose to live freely.

"Number Thirty-seven: *'o monaco* (The Monk). Today a monk, from Jerusalem, told me that faith is a gift, because it eases pain and nourishes hope. It's not opium, but concrete help. God recognises you, he knows your pain, he's by your side, helping to bring relief. It's the hand that lifts you when you fall, that says, 'I'm here, don't be afraid, all this will pass, I'll help you get up and, if you can't, I'll help you face what is to come. There are no miracles, the only miracle we can work is the one on ourselves, the miracle of not always seeing the worst, of seeing the light in the dark.'"

"I see a light in the dark too," interrupted the coffee pot. "It's almost dawn."

"They'll be coming for us soon. The other truck already emptied the organic waste. We'll be next. At least without that stench, I can breathe again - in fact, I can smell coffee."

"That's me, Notebook, dear. I told you, they threw me in here half full."

Drops of coffee splashed the open pages of the notebook, forming the number forty-two. "Thanks, for being a friend, for being there, for being one of her last thoughts too," the coffee pot added.

"No, thank you, Coffee Pot, for allowing me to savour your sincere friendship. Life is a chain, it's the survival of the fittest, all you can do is accept the end and rely on the good Lord. We'll meet again, I know we will, somehow we'll find a way to 'exist' again. My pages will turn yellow, like the petals of a yellow rose, and you will become its scent. We'll always belong to *Signora* Rosa, so look out for me. I'll send you a sign, you'll recognise me and smile and I'll recognise you and be happy. Even if we're something else, we'll still be wonderful. Don't be afraid. We'll take one last breath, close our eyes and let them take us away. It will be like taking an afternoon nap. Our lives may be over, but life will go on as usual, and may our next lives be better than our last. Goodbye, my friend!"

And so the two friends bid farewell. Their imaginations

had taken them beyond the confines of the rubbish skip to new horizons. Their dreams had suddenly become real, so real that they hardly notice the refuse truck, come to take them away to be recycled.

The Red Rose -
The Diary of my Imperfections

Writing can be great therapy. It helps overcome mental blocks and fears, helps us gain self-awareness, giving voice to our imperfections, to repressed memories, to our discomfort, to the burdens we carry inside us which have no other way out, entrusting them to a distant friend, who perhaps doesn't even

know us in person, who has the key to interpreting them, identifying with us: the reader.

Dear Readers,

If, given the circumstances, you find I'm speaking out of context or expressing myself inadequately, if I don't give the right answers to your questions, please, don't judge me. Or, if you really have to, try not to do it before you've read these pages from my diary.

I live with imperfection, and it's also my greatest fear. It undresses me shamelessly, pitilessly, laying bare my shortcomings to the world. Leaving me looking silly, ridiculous, or, if it's feeling generous, simply unsuitable for purpose. I'm used to it now, and wait, motionless, no longer capable of surprise or hope. If there's something special inside me, it will never be revealed or, if it is, it will be deformed, because forcing it to reveal itself will damage it and my self-esteem.

It's as if gagged, my hands tied, my feet bound, someone suddenly told me to run. It's impossible. I try, but I look comical and clumsy. If I don't give up, I realise that all I'm doing is publicly projecting my imperfections and not what I want to project. So I take refuge in mediocrity, identifying myself with a paralysed yet comfortable image, which has become my default response to everything. I know it doesn't represent the real me, I'm quite different but, at the moment, it's the only painless existence I know. My physical appearance, for want of a euphemism, doesn't help: a small, bulbous nose, a mouth that's just a little too full, round eyes with a permanent red cyst on my upper left eyelid, cellulite that makes my thighs look like two huge saddlebags and, last but not least, a series of irregular dark moles scattered willy-nilly all over my body like a leopard's spots.

That's me, no more, no less: an imperfect being in search of perfection, who fails constantly and never gets back on their feet. I won't dwell on my physical imperfections however, they're the ones that hurt the least. Mostly, I feel like a human rubbish bin, filled with refuse, crawling with bugs and cockroaches.

My first encounter with imperfection was when I discovered my "speech anxiety", an irreversible imprinting with no way out. Some define it as a form of Tourette's with tics, others an acute form of SAD. I don't know what it was, but I do know that it felt like my body and mind were blocked, as if a huge spotlight had stopped me in my tracks, highlighting all my defects and showing them off to everyone who was present.

I couldn't speak – inside, my voice was clear and perfect, my speech flowed smoothly, but I couldn't get it out. I suddenly started to gulp, my face twitched, my head jerked then, finally, I gave a huge cough, and one single vowel came out, that I repeated endlessly, on a loop, and I've no idea why. I was possessed by something rhythmic and obsessive, uncontrollable, that, try as I might, was just the first in a long series of deadlocks. I knew perfectly well what I wanted to say, I'd been over my speech several times, carefully studying the details, going over the vital parts. I was proud of it... but nothing, not one word, came out. Then, the palpitations began, my heart beating furiously, like an out of control drum. I blushed, my face scarlet with shame, glistening and soaked with drops of cold sweat that refused to dry. I couldn't swallow, my mouth was like a desert, my tongue glued to the roof of my mouth. Trembling and shaking, all I wanted to do was disappear - melt, or even better, dissolve into a gaseous state and float away forever.

And all the time he was staring at me, judging me, smirking. I'll never forget the smug look on the face of that middle-aged guy, trying so hard to look young in his hipster glasses: a cheap, two-bit lawyer, who I'd previously been indifferent to but, in the blink of an eye, had now earned my undying hatred. Though I seemed helpless and distant, I could clearly hear his sneered, sarcastic jokes, pseudo-humour based on mockery, dispensed from the height of his universal knowledge and wisdom. He seemed hostile, distant, an enemy. And I wanted to hit him, with all my strength, with the first thing that came to hand, but I just stood there, completely paralysed. He was enjoying my failure, mercilessly watching me sink even further, haughty and irritating, with a superficial, know-it-all sneer, casually flaunting his evil presumptuousness in front of everyone. He seemed to take great pleasure in knowing I'd lost it, that I was so inferior, too weak and unable to defend myself or even walk away. He did nothing to show support or ease my discomfort. He looked like one of those hyenas, the ones whose teeth are always exposed in an absurd grin, who devour the carcasses of already dead animals without having to make the effort to capture them. I immediately understood what I was dealing with: a piece of shit disguised as an intellectual.

From then on, I swore I'd never speak in public again and if I had no choice, I'd make sure I read, even better, that someone else read, something that I'd prepared in advance. As for the laughing lawyer, who for professional reasons I was forced to meet occasionally, I decided to give him the treatment he deserved: privately cursing him from behind my sneer, just like the one he gave me - curses, which if they ever came true, would have made his life literally impossible. I cursed him with my eyes, silently expressing all the rage and resentment I felt for him with an icy glare.

I imagined him in various uncomfortable situations; speaking in public with a piece of spinach stuck between his teeth or with his flies undone - even worse, with an upset stomach, his guts gurgling while he tried to hold in noxious intestinal gases. I imagined him sweating, stammering, trembling, red-faced, a tiny being, like a Lilliputian. When I heard he'd started suffering from sudden migraines on both sides of his head, I was overjoyed. His pain intensified every time I stared at him. His eyes became intolerant to light, and I noticed he couldn't stand noise or smells. He began to lose his aplomb and that extreme nonchalance. Had I infected him with my imperfection? Had I transmitted it to him telepathically, through brain-to-brain communication. I wanted him to be exposed. I didn't want anyone feeling sorry for him. I wanted his awkward, superficial soul to be stripped naked and ugly before everyone, like it had been for me.

After my very public mortification, I was diagnosed with a severe form of glossophobia, a social disease which was very hard to cure and probably linked to latent experiences that I'd removed from my consciousness. I refused any form of therapy, abandoning any priorities linked to social relations. I decided to face my disease alone, if anyone was capable of immersing themselves in the chaos that was my mind, it was me. The only way I could achieve that was through writing, about myself, which meant moving out of myself and looking down from the outside. Becoming my own therapist, no longer my saboteur, my own worst enemy. I was going to have to get to know my enemy, by analysing it under a microscope, like a scientist examining a dangerous virus. By changing perspective, observing myself from the outside, I would perhaps have caused that countertransference that would have allowed me to carefully mend my wounds and carry out some delicate embroidery that I would have shown only to honest and sensitive eyes. Only by watching, listening and understanding myself, would I find a way out of this internal self-sabotage.

And all the time I found myself making liberating notes about people and events that had left me emotionally scarred, the ones who had sucked my energy mercilessly, who'd transferred their negative and depressing thoughts to me, or those who'd sneakily tried to put me down, discrediting my work, destroying my plans, lying, or shaming me in public by blurting out my weaknesses or secrets in front of everyone.

From this chaotic vortex of my emotions, a cathartic diary of my imperfections was born.

Cleopatra is the first emotional baggage I want to off load. She made me and she still has the power to hurt me. It's time to get rid of her forever, because hers is the first face that brings back bad memories.

The Cleopatra I'm referring to has nothing in common with the beautiful Egyptian Queen, apart from the more harmful aspects. The Cleopatra I intend removing from my mind is an arrogant country bumpkin version, whose peasant nature is revealed by her constant bowing and scraping. In the whirlwind of my emotions, Cleopatra appears before me, boastful, arrogant and extremely cunning. Aesthetically, she looks like a lumpy sack of potatoes with a clump of straw sticking out of the top. Victim of her own ambitions, she always insists on being at the centre of attention, stealing the scene, and the credit of others, shamelessly screaming and demanding applause, whether she deserves it or not.

I associate her with a terrifying echo that goes on and on indefinitely, repeating the same mnemonic and tedious phrases over and over, which, though grammatically correct, are flat and arouse no emotion just annoyance. She surrounds herself with Yes men, who indulge her with their lies (certainly not for her own good) pretending to appreciate her, flattering her, revering her, then ridiculing her behind her back. Poor Cleopatra! They tear her apart with their nasty sharp knives, mercilessly attacking her. With her I relive my worst splatter film (a genre I never liked), in which Cleopatra's blood spurts everywhere and her insides spill out of her body. I feel disgusted. Her killers surround her. I hate her, yet I also pity her.

I often have an image of Cleopatra face to face with an insurmountable obstacle: she cries, she's desperate. She accuses me unfairly, overwhelming me. Hoping to get the better of me, she pretends to be my victim, then attacks me from behind, taking my place, saying it's hers. She returns, bold, competitive, shamelessly brash and, above all, a liar. She's a natural liar, she does it all the time, even to herself. She'll insist that black is white, then, when she's sure everyone agrees with her, she pouts smugly.

The same pout she uses in official photos, or when she's trying to seduce someone, but most of all, when she's trying to manipulate others. The pout makes her look like a real asshole - one of those rich in E. Coli and other bacteria, which produces foul-smelling excreta. In other words, she's full of shit!

Spoiled, capricious, never satisfied, prone to intrigues and with the kind of ego that demands continuous flattery and tries to transform her followers into copies of herself. I hear the sycophantic fawning - the words of her killers, and smell the stench of their rancid insincerity. I need to cast her memory from my mind. It's a corpse in advanced state of putrefaction. I need to lay it to rest forever. By eliminating her, erasing her and everything that surrounds her from my mind, I find that I've freed up so much space in my memory and saved a lot of energy.

The second image that haunts me, in various forms, is that of Ella. I've known Ella since I was born. She's always considered me a second-rate member of the family and from behind her facade of respectable, devout churchgoer, she's never done anything to hide it. It's her fault if I prefer the company of sinners, those who make mistakes because they're open about their passions, their hate, their love, their anger. Ella lied to herself and to me and I've never been able to understand why.

Without knowing anything about me, without even knowing me, she judged me. She already knew everything about me, so what else was there to find out? There was nothing I was ever going to do to change her mind. Her mind was made up - I was imperfect. Someone to ignore, to avoid. To throw away.

At first, I wanted to prove her wrong. I tried everything to make her notice me, to see that I existed. That there was something good in me. She demolished me with her indifference, comparing me to others in the most negative terms – worse, she seemed to enjoy it.

I couldn't understand and wondered: why am I imperfect? Why can't she accept me? Why won't she even give me a chance? I exist too and I want to show her I do. What do they have more than me? If I'm not good enough for her, why doesn't she help me improve?

It was so hard! Yet, she prayed to God. Said she was religious - but she was as hard as stone, like a rock. If you came up against her, you were the one who got hurt. She was full of secrets. She enjoyed hinting that there were things she didn't want me to know, keeping me in the dark about her world, where entrance was reserved to her chosen few. It was a real effort for her to talk to me, and if she really had to, she only said absurd, meaningless things, or praised someone else just to put me down. She didn't want me anywhere near her son, so talking to him was totally out of the question. The poor kid was so scared that one day he even refused to give me a lift on his scooter. He preferred giving a ride to some stranger, who didn't have low blood pressure like me. I had to walk all the way home, in the hot sun, at the risk of fainting, of feeling sick. But I saw the look on his face, how my pleas and requests for help made him suffer. He knew he was making a mistake, that it was wrong, but he preferred to listen to his mother than his own conscience. She was his God.

I never forgave him for that. I finally saw him for who he was. If I was a loser, then he was a wimp, with no personality and no freedom of spirit, a useless chicken who didn't have the guts to do the right thing.

A thousand times I wondered - Who am I exactly? Am I really that bad? What am I doing wrong? Why all this hostility towards me?

Ella made me feel like scum, a good for nothing, a runt, an outcast. But I wasn't, I'm not, I never have been - and I wasn't interested in her son in the slightest. And even if I was, just remember how Jesus treated a woman, who for Ella would be just a cheap slut, who crouched before him, washing his feet with her tears, kissing them with all the love she had to give. He didn't judge her. He could read her heart. He knew how much she loved him by the pureness of her extraordinary gesture. Why couldn't Ella be like him and imitate the actions of her Lord and Saviour?

Whenever Ella was around, I felt repugnant and insecure. I'd tried everything to prove her wrong, but nothing, her attitude just got worse. I started to hate her and wish her all the bad luck she deserved. I gave up and decided to let her think what she wanted, pretending to accept the fact that when it came to her hateful ideas of perfection, I was decidedly inferior.

Ella was my enemy, a stranger. I couldn't stand the sight of her. I began to ignore her, avoiding her whenever I could. Every time I saw her, I felt sick. She literally made me wretch. My body refused her like disgusting, rotten food. Her absence felt like a liberation. I had to eliminate her from my life, she was a toxic substance from which my body and mind defended themselves. Whenever I bumped into her, it set alarm bells ringing inside me that put me into flight mode.

It's time to make room, clear my memories of her forever: a full-blown space clearing, mental purification, cancelling the things that prevent me from being happy, or at least from feeling free.

From my mental chaos, another dark image emerges, and I make out the face of the person my mind calls The Manipulator.

The Manipulator is an enigmatic figure with a dual personality, who scares me, giving me nightmares that keep me awake at night.

When I first met him, he was the exact opposite of what he later turned out to be. With deception and lies, with a skilfully created romance scam, he earned my trust.

We shared the same hobbies, interests and passions, and he came across as very likeable, compatible with my flaws and, most of all, empathic. With an all-out charm offensive, he manipulated me masterfully until he gained my total trust and left me defenceless. The first thing that comes to mind is the way he enforced his power, preventing me from expressing myself, which restricted my language skills, limiting them to tried and tested sentences, which I knew wouldn't irritate or provoke him.

The Manipulator brought out the very worst in me. He took my happiness, my light-heartedness, and threw them away forever. He liked to keep me awake at night, for ridiculous reasons, for the anger inside himself that he wanted to transfer to me, to make me feel as bad as him, or simply to undermine me. If I didn't say anything he'd provoke me, torture me, trying to get me to react, then hurt me and tell me to shut up. He made me pray, forcing me down on my knees, to beg forgiveness for my countless sins. He wanted me to confess them out loud and if they were mild, or not the ones he was thinking of, he'd scream and yell and tell me not to lie. To placate him, I had to say what he wanted me to say but his mind was so contorted that it was hard to know exactly what he wanted to hear.

When it came to highlighting my defects, especially the

physical ones, he was an expert. He'd do it with such anger, such cunning, such spite, that I felt completely worthless. I wanted to get away from him forever, or at least to close my eyes and fall asleep and escape the nightmare I was living.

My life was over. I was at the end of the line. I no longer lived in the world, but in a hell where he was my ruler, my commander, my oppressor. He was Lucifer and I was some poor devil. I'd given him my soul and now the doors of Heaven were closed to me. There was no escape from his violence. He used it as a tool to silence me, to prevent me from saying anything that could make him feel uncomfortable or upset him.

I let myself go, I was run down, just skin and bone. I was tired, but I couldn't leave. In establishing a pseudo-peaceful relationship with him, I'd given up on myself, on my aspirations, my innate light-heartedness. In my obedience to him, I'd cancelled forever any attempts at critical thinking. I accepted whatever he wanted. I was an automaton with a hypocritical semblance of submission. It was the price I paid for a few hours peace, when I could be myself, instead of how he wanted me to be. That was the extent of his psychological manipulation and the hold he had over me.

Once I was totally dependent on him, The Manipulator left me. His work was done. It was time to move on, to find another victim to manipulate. He disappeared. I let him think I was heart-broken. I knew him well enough to know it was the only way to keep him from coming back, that it would boost his ego even more: he'd brought his mission to an excellent conclusion. In reality, his abandonment felt as if the steel chain around my neck had finally snapped.

I left the place of my confinement. I ran outside and rolled in the mud like a pig trying to cool down and eliminate parasites.

Because he was a parasite. Slowly and surely, he had taken possession of me, causing me sickness and exhaustion, making me tired of life.

Now I was pressing the 'delete' button, permanently eliminating the face that no longer hurt me.

I needed to dig down deeper. I still hadn't got to the bottom of my chaos, there was still so much more to get out.

I recognised the face of a childhood friend: Nale. Why was she so far down in my memories? Because it was a long time ago, when I was maybe four, five years old.

Nale was a couple of years older than me. I looked up to her. She knew how to do so many things, and all of them better than me. I'd watch her playing hopscotch on the square of concrete in front of our building, and she never put a foot wrong. With a stone we'd draw a series of squares. I'd watch as she tossed the stone into the first square, never missing, then hopped forward, balancing on one leg in the single squares, on two feet in the double squares, hopping and skipping, making her way along the squares without once touching the outlines or losing her balance. Once she finished, she'd start all over again, never making a mistake - which meant that I never got a turn. She always won, hopping all the way to the end and back without her other foot touching the ground.

I'm not envious or jealous, so why was she here, living in my chaos? I look closer, trying to focus, and blurred, indefinable memories start to emerge. Residual memories that only now I start to understand as they slowly take shape, becoming bad memories that I had totally removed. Nale abuses me. She touches me where I don't want to be touched, where no one should touch me, pushing, hurting. She covers my mouth so I can't scream. Why won't she stop? I don't like it, it hurts, I feel sick, ashamed. I don't want to do it but I'm helpless, defenceless. She's won. She always does, she's stronger than me. When we're alone she always makes me do what she wants. I don't want to be alone with her. I told my mother, but she wouldn't listen, she says I have to play with children my own age, not stay with the adults, if I want to grow up properly.

I want to throw the hopscotch stone at her and run away. I want to hurt her like she hurt me, but my body won't move. I see her big, hateful face, that smug grin; she enjoys what she does to me. I have no choice. I have to find the courage to resist and put off my rebellion for another day. When I'm older, I'll make her pay. I'll win at hopscotch and I'll never let her touch me again.

I'm shivering. I'm drenched in cold sweat, shaking. It's my body's reaction to the repressed memory. All those years I kept it hidden and now it won't go away. I have to delete it forever. It has to go. It doesn't belong to me anymore.

I see myself at nursery school. Silent. The other kids are

laughing. They think I can't speak, that there's something wrong with me, that I'm trying to hide some stutter or that my vocabulary is too limited because I'm not like them - I haven't practised my reading ten times like them, reading out loud, and I haven't learned the new words. I don't speak because I'm afraid they won't understand me. I'm afraid to scream the pain and rage that I have inside me, which I cannot describe in words. My mind is resilient. It's built a high, protective barrier. It won't give in, and it won't allow me to express myself. Before it's too late, I press the delete button, but the memory is still there.

I see a nun, all dressed in black. She becomes a crow with a human voice. Holding a rod in her beak, she lashes out at me, screaming, yelling at me to recite the multiplication tables from memory. She pushes me down until I'm kneeling on rice sprinkled behind the blackboard. My knees hurt, they're bleeding. Everyone laughs, insulting me. I pass out from pain and shame. Angrily, I press the delete button and black feathers flutter all around me, together with numbers from the multiplication tables. There's so much confusion around me, I'm scared now. I don't want to dig further. I can't stand it, I can't write any more. My past memories and the pain they bring with them, are becoming too harmful, no longer therapeutic.

I can't dig any further right now, perhaps in the future, when I'm feeling better. I see my past, I relive it, moment by moment, feeling sensations that are not totally unknown to me. The abreaction is too much. I'll never be able to cleanse my body and soul of all the past contaminations, of my inner evils. Everything will remain dark and unacceptable chaos. I have to stop and accept my imperfections before I go crazy. I need something to take me far away from here.

I see a beautiful red rose that stands out among the other flowers, for its beauty, its perfection, its scent. I reach out and pick it, holding it tight. My hands hurt, they're bleeding. That's when I notice the soft, prickly growths on the stem that make it imperfect, just like me. They make me love it even more and I squeeze it tighter.

In a few days, it will wither and die and my old scars will disappear, perhaps giving way to new ones.

All of reality is imperfection, everything that surrounds me, even what to me seems perfect, is incapable of evading the laws of change and transience. So why do I get so angry? Why am I so afraid of my imperfections? Maybe I should learn to embrace my uniqueness. My scars would no longer be from my failures, my defeats, but from my capacity to reinvent myself, my resilience.

So now you know the secret of my misfortune, please don't make it public property. Try and understand me and, if you can, try to be a little kinder, more generous. By helping me, you'll learn to help yourself if you're unlucky enough to come face to face with your imperfections and a monstrous chaos you're unable to name.

Rose Rose –
The Romance Scam

The need for affection, to feel love, to be acknowledged, the search for our other half, to feel complete, is sometimes so strong that we give into the illusion, to the magic of the fairy tale, taking flight without wings, which inevitably leaves us lying wounded on the ground. Some say, however, that what counts is the not the landing, but that brief moment when it feels like you're flying.

Rose Rose – the Romance Scam

Rose Rose had just turned fifty. She wasn't beautiful. She wasn't ugly either. Immediately after qualifying as an accountant, she'd started work in her uncle's factory, where she spent more than twelve hours a day in a tiny room, balancing the books in exchange for a meager salary, which she never complained about. She spent all day at work and, in the evening after a frugal meal, she went straight to bed. The next day, she woke up, went to work and started all over again, exactly where she'd left off.

On Sunday, her only day off, she'd go to church then to the supermarket at the shopping centre, after which she'd prepare an entire meal of slow food, which she savoured with gusto (unlike during the week) then she'd clean the house: organising her wardrobe, doing the ironing and the housework she'd ignored all week, until her eyes drooped from exhaustion and she went to bed.

In the capsule of her existence, a pre-established order reigned supreme. Rose had always been like a hamster, running furiously on its wheel without once stopping to wonder why, she just did it. She had never felt like a woman with a capital 'W', with hopes and desires and, most of all, she had never felt the weight of solitude: she was too busy with balance sheets and budgets.

When her uncle had come down with Covid 19, infecting her in the process, she'd been forced to quarantine. Once better, she intended to work remotely. The problem was, she felt like a stranger in her own home. She wasn't used to being in her apartment during the day. She was used to the twenty square-metres of her office, no windows, no balcony, and no one for company but the constant presence of her uncle, the accounts and her spread sheets. It was her home/her prison and beyond those confines, she felt like a stranger in a strange land.

The company had loaned her a top of the range computer with super-fast internet connection so she could work and transmit data to her uncle in real time.

Her apartment felt like a non-place, however, and it was like spending the whole day in unfamiliar surroundings. For the first time, Rose began to experience loneliness, or perhaps it was more an emptiness that she badly needed to fill. One day, she found herself browsing idly through the icons on the desktop of her computer. After a while, she clicked on the Facebook icon, only because blue was her favourite colour, although she always wore grey.

When it opened, she read through the instructions then, following them to the letter, like she always did, she set up her profile, completing it with a selfie - but only after she'd combed her hair, applied a little lipstick and put on her best blouse.

She looked at the screen. She liked what she saw, though it all seemed a little strange, transgressive even. Now she existed in virtual reality too and she wasn't wearing grey. She was wearing her best blue blouse and plum lipstick. "Rose Rose, accountant. Single."

She explored the pages and profiles that had things in common with her, curious to see if there was anyone she knew or was connected to the company. Suddenly a pinging noise distracted her. She checked the icon in the corner: a friend request.

'Who on earth is White Knight? What a funny name! Obviously not his real name - or is it? No, his surname's either White, or Knight... not everyone is as lucky as me. At least with my name there's no confusion!'

Without knowing who the White Knight was or why he'd suddenly appeared, Rose Rose, decided to accept. She didn't have many friends. To tell the truth, she didn't have any, she didn't have the time. Her mother, who'd been unmarried, had died giving birth to her, and she'd been brought up by her elderly grandmother, of whom she remembered very little.

Her grandmother, who had no imagination whatsoever, had given her the same name as her surname: Rose. When her grandmother died, Rose had been taken in by her uncle, her mother's younger brother, who had raised her, sent her to college, then given her a job.

Her uncle, a somewhat solitary person, was also extremely devoid of affection. He'd never been in a relationship and continued to live alone with only his housekeepers for company, who were replaced whenever they made demands or became too curious. Rose hadn't lived with him since she turned eighteen - her uncle had insisted she move out and live alone in the ground floor apartment of his building.

The apartment was her uncle's gift for her eighteenth birthday. Rose didn't know why, but she never questioned her uncle's decisions, and always showed obsequious devotion to him.

He made sure she had everything she needed, as long as

and no one for company but the constant presence of her uncle, the accounts and her spread sheets. It was her home/her prison and beyond those confines, she felt like a stranger in a strange land.

The company had loaned her a top of the range computer with super-fast internet connection so she could work and transmit data to her uncle in real time.

Her apartment felt like a non-place, however, and it was like spending the whole day in unfamiliar surroundings. For the first time, Rose began to experience loneliness, or perhaps it was more an emptiness that she badly needed to fill. One day, she found herself browsing idly through the icons on the desktop of her computer. After a while, she clicked on the Facebook icon, only because blue was her favourite colour, although she always wore grey.

When it opened, she read through the instructions then, following them to the letter, like she always did, she set up her profile, completing it with a selfie - but only after she'd combed her hair, applied a little lipstick and put on her best blouse.

She looked at the screen. She liked what she saw, though it all seemed a little strange, transgressive even. Now she existed in virtual reality too and she wasn't wearing grey. She was wearing her best blue blouse and plum lipstick. "Rose Rose, accountant. Single."

She explored the pages and profiles that had things in common with her, curious to see if there was anyone she knew or was connected to the company. Suddenly a pinging noise distracted her. She checked the icon in the corner: a friend request.

'Who on earth is White Knight? What a funny name! Obviously not his real name - or is it? No, his surname's either White, or Knight... not everyone is as lucky as me. At least with my name there's no confusion!'

Without knowing who the White Knight was or why he'd suddenly appeared, Rose Rose, decided to accept. She didn't have many friends. To tell the truth, she didn't have any, she didn't have the time. Her mother, who'd been unmarried, had died giving birth to her, and she'd been brought up by her elderly grandmother, of whom she remembered very little.

Her grandmother, who had no imagination whatsoever, had given her the same name as her surname: Rose. When her grandmother died, Rose had been taken in by her uncle, her mother's younger brother, who had raised her, sent her to college, then given her a job.

Her uncle, a somewhat solitary person, was also extremely devoid of affection. He'd never been in a relationship and continued to live alone with only his housekeepers for company, who were replaced whenever they made demands or became too curious. Rose hadn't lived with him since she turned eighteen - her uncle had insisted she move out and live alone in the ground floor apartment of his building.

The apartment was her uncle's gift for her eighteenth birthday. Rose didn't know why, but she never questioned her uncle's decisions, and always showed obsequious devotion to him.

He made sure she had everything she needed, as long as

she didn't need anything he considered "superfluous", which for him meant a little gift, a weekend away, a trip to the cinema or anything else that wasn't connected to the world of working. He wasn't a bad person, he simply lacked the capacity to love, to express and feel emotions. No one had ever taught him to love, and it was the same with Rose.

- Hello, Mr. White Knight. Do I know you?
- Nice to meet you, Rose Rose. I'm the White Knight, a nickname, obviously. I use it online, it suits me better than my real name.
- Why? Do you work with white horses?
- No! Of course not. I'm a knight, as in shining armour. Are you familiar with the *Puellae* Code?
- Is that Latin? I'm an accountant, and Latin isn't on the curriculum.
- No, it's not Latin...if you let me explain, it will help you understand who I really am. I'll send you a sample of the code and you'll seehow it expresses my true nature:

  I. Respect women, always help a damsel in distress.
  II. If you care about a lady's heart, become her champion, take part in tournaments, always support her honour.
  III. Do not deliberately cause trouble when a lady is in a relationship with someone else.
- All that? What do you get out of it?
- I do it for the pure enjoyment. I love it. When my woman is happy, I'm happy. I'm a free spirit looking for love and a lady, a beautiful, graceful lady like you, Rose Rose.
- You don't even know me!
- Forgive me, but I know you better than you think. One look at your profile pic and your eyes spoke to me. They

told me they want to be loved, that you are probably my other half.
- Really? You got all that from a simple selfie? And what do you mean, "other half"? We don't even know each other!
- I have the power to understand whoever I meet, from the first glance. Let me call you Rose, Rose. I see your soul and I know it's lonely. You're looking for me too, you just don't know it yet.
- All right, White Knight, you can call me Rose, but I'll say goodbye now. I've heard enough. I'll speak to you some other time, perhaps.
- I'll wait for you tomorrow evening, at the same time, Rose Rose. Don't be late, don't make me wait.

That night Rose couldn't sleep. All she could think about was the White Knight, he'd taken the place of all those numbers, spread sheets and income and expenditure calculations. She pictured him on his white horse, handsome, charming, with Asian features, a foreigner but from where? Out of billions of people, why had he chosen her? She'd never heard such kind words from anyone before. Suddenly, she felt like a Woman, no longer a human calculator, an infallible machine.

Her self-esteem improved and she took great pleasure in fantasising about what her future held.

She counted the hours, the minutes, the seconds, until it was time for their second appointment. She logged into her account and opened the chat.

- Hi, there, Rose Rose. I couldn't wait to hear from you. It felt like time had stood still. Without you I'm lost, alone

in the middle of an infinite ocean.
- You talk about the ocean and I've never even seen the sea. I went to the lake once with my grandmother, but I was too young to remember much. I'd like to see the ocean.
- Don't talk like that, Rose Rose! You're spoiling the romance.
- I didn't mean to. You see, I've never even been out of my city. I've never seen other countries or rivers, lakes or seas. I've led a very restricted life and my little world is the only world I know. What about you, White Knight? Have you travelled? Have you seen the world?
- I'm never in the same place twice, continually searching for my lady, exploring every remote corner. Now I think I've found the right place, your little world.
- And what's your world like?
- My world has no horizons. I navigate the ether and now you're navigating it with me. So you see, you're little world isn't so small anymore. In any case, I don't live too far from you, but I'm away at the moment, on business.
- Can I ask what you look like, since you don't have any photos on your profile?
- I'm just as you see me in your imagination, nothing more, nothing less.
- That's a little vague. You could be anyone. You haven't even been clear about who you are in real life and, most of all, what you want from me.
- You'll find out in good time, but only if you want to listen to me and get to know me. I just want you to know that every time we say goodbye, I die a little. I love you in the dark, secretly, and I can't wait to see you up close. I really hope you feel the same way.

Rose Rose and the White Knight always met online at the same time, 7.30pm. Exactly thirty minutes later, without ever going one second over, the chat would suddenly end and they'd agree to meet again the next evening. It was always the Knight who ended the conversation, saying he had to get back to work.

Rose Rose noticed however, that the White Knight always remained online, even if he was no longer chatting to her.

At first she didn't mind, but then she felt her heart beating - the White Knight had awakened her abstract idea of love and she grew suspicious.

They chatted exclusively on Facebook. Rose Rose logged in every evening at the appointed time however, the White Knight's behaviour was different. One day, she logged in earlier than usual and was surprised to see the green dot on his profile - he was already online. She waited a few moments then opened the chat, but he didn't answer. He completely ignored her and Rose couldn't understand why.

She made careful note of when he was online - she kept a spreadsheet of when and what time. There were certain times when he was always active. What was he doing spending all that time online without his lady? Why hadn't he replied to her message? He'd been online. Why hadn't he noticed her? Why hadn't he said anything? He hadn't even explained. Rose knew they were both adults and could do whatever they wanted without having to ask the other's permission, but if he loved her as much as he said he did, then he owed her an explanation.

When it was time for their usual chat, after saying hi, Rose asked the question that had been on her mind.

- For the past few days I've been logging in early and saw that you were already online. I tried to chat with you once you but you never replied.
- My beautiful one, you know how it is. Sometimes I leave the computer running for hours, even when I'm not around. If I didn't answer it's simply because I wasn't there. My dear Rose, I want to be with you all the time and if I'm not it's because something has cropped up. What I want most in life is to be with you, always, you know that.

Rose Rose didn't reply, but she wasn't satisfied. Before she could believe him, she needed tangible, concrete evidence, and found that she'd suddenly become jealous and suspicious. So suspicious that she decided to create another account, under another name: Linda Azzurri, receptionist, single. She chose a profile pic from the internet, a copyright-free photo of a good-looking woman around her own age. Then she searched the White Knight's friend list. She discovered that his friends were almost exclusively women her own age, all single. There were no posts on his profile, no profile pictures, no information about his work or family, and nothing that gave her any clues about his likes or his habits.

She decided to take things further and, very daringly, sent him a friend request. He probably won't even see it, she thought, he'll be too busy working to even notice it. But she was wrong...

After only a couple of seconds, she noticed that not only had he accepted her friend request, he was already interacting with her fictitious "alt".

She was jealous. Mostly, she was disappointed, but she decided to ignore it and play along. The Knight had very little imagination - everything he wrote was copy and paste of everything he'd written to her. She knew his words so well, they were the ones that kept her awake at night, fantasising.

After thirty minutes, just as she'd expected, he said goodbye to Linda Azzurri and, just like he'd done with her that first time, suggested a time to meet up in chat.

Rose Rose's world came crashing down. The only love of her life was fake, a sham, a phoney. She'd been catfished.

What was she going to do now? What would become of her? She'd have to go back to eating, or watching TV, or working - worthless expedients, no longer capable of making her feel fulfilled. She wasn't the same as before and she knew it, there was no going back now. If she was going to get rid of her pain, to let it all out, she'd have to learn to make room for it.

Just like she did at work, she looked at it from a financial point of view, doing an in-depth cost-benefits analysis of what had just happened. She had two options - she could close her account or she could carry on and make the most of it. After careful consideration, she reached her decision: she decided to continue the game, but to play by her own rules. After all, she thought, if I went to a psychologist, I've have to pay him to listen to me –and the White Knight listened to her. He made her feel good and was completely free. She didn't care if he was telling the truth or not. His words gratified her, they made her life magical, or at least, less dreary. So why split hairs?So, Rose Rose decided to create a whole series of fake, female, profiles, so she could chat with the White Knight when she most wanted. She always used the same technique to lure him in - she sent him a friend request, which he accepted in a matter of seconds, then he'd contact her and away they'd go, always the same script.

One day, the White Knight asked her for a loan. A small sum of money, so he could come and see her, spend some time with her. His business wasn't going too well and he couldn't afford to fulfill his dream of meeting her in person.

Rose knew she shouldn't have done it, but she couldn't help it. She wanted to give him one last chance. He'd listened to her, made her feel good, woken her from her hibernation, and meeting him would be a dream come true. If it was all an illusion and he disappeared with her money, she wouldn't be offended however, it was a small sum of money and the White Knight had earned his fee. He'd given her his time, made her feel emotions and, as they said in business, time was money.

- Thank you, my darling Rose. It's just a temporary loan, to help me get my affairs in order. I'lljoin you as soon as I can.
- You know, White Knight, your words sound almost like a farewell. Life is full of formidable adventures and I'm

sure you're about to embark on a new one, then another, and another. Good luck for the future and goodbye.

Rose bid him farewell. In her heart she already knew that once he received her money, she'd never hear from him again. And that's what happened. The White Knight continued to be online - she saw his green dot - but he never contacted her again. Rose didn't ask for explanations. Instead, she became Linda Azzurri, then Ortensia Civarri, Roberta Stregiavalle and many more. When, true to his script, the Knight asked for money, Rose Rose's alt either disappeared or she asked him to wait, to be patient, she was a little short of cash at the moment but would soon be in receipt of a large sum of money. It was always the same - a simple way of establishing contact with other humans, and it saw Rose through the entire lockdown period.

When it was time to get back to her usual routine, back to her little world, Rose realised that not only Covid 19 was over, but so was that strange desire to be a Woman with a capital W, which had accompanied her throughout the pandemic. She went back to her life as an accountant, back to her twenty square-metres.

And she realised that it was the only thing she really liked, the only thing that gave her satisfaction.

About the Author

Maria Tedeschi teaches English Language and Culture at the *Liceo Classico Plinio Seniore* in Castellammare di Stabia in Naples, Italy. She is the school's internationalisation and international mobility coordinator, in charge of English language public relations with China.

Two years ago she was nominated Kindness Ambassador for the *Cor et Amor* association in Ivrea and has made kindness her life's philosophy.

Passionate about travel, rock music and literature, she lives in Sant'Antonio Abate, Naples, with her husband, Aldo, and their two children, Domenico and Maria Grazia Azzurra.

She loves storytelling and, together with her students, has made several short films[1], some also in English, which have

---

[1] Best Short Film, at CineCibo, 2011, with soundtrack by Eugenio Bennato. Technical Jury Award for Best Short Film - Senior Category (High Schools) at Cinefrutta 2012, soundtrack by the English band, Gold Skies Ahead.
Gold Medal in the 2017/2017 "Premiazione del Concorso Nazionale L'Archivio Nazionale dei Monumenti Adottati dalle scuole Italiane "Villa S. Marco, l'adottiamo noi!", with a soundtrack self-produced in collaboration with the rapper Dominas.

won first place or the gold medal in several national competitions.

She made her writing debut with "*Non chiudere quella porta*", published by Iseafbooks, which received several awards, including an honorable mention in the second edition of the "Amore sui Generis" literary awards.

The was followed by "*La Maiastra e le vite invisibili*", her second book, winner of the 2021 International Literature Award at the Italian Cultural Institute of Naples. The novel was also selected by Casa Sanremo for its 2023 writers' edition.

As a songwriter, she has collaborated with several bands, both Italian and English. The Rose Trilogy, in Italian and English, is her latest literary effort. The first story in the trilogy, "The Yellow Rose" is already available on Audible as a gift for the visually impaired, and the French translation is featured in a literary anthology.

Gold Medal in the 2017/2018 "Premiazione del Concorso Nazionale L'Archivio Nazionale dei Monumenti Adottati dalle scuole italiane" for the video "Via Coppola and her Secrets", with soundtrack by the rapper Nto.

Afterword

Why an English version?

The contemporary psycholinguist Frank Smith once said, "One language sets you in a corridor for life. Two languages open every door along the way."

This is extraordinarily true, in the sense that "translating" means "ethically transferring" a text from one language to another. Unfortunately, in our fast-paced and superficial world, we often rely on Google Translate, then declare ourselves polyglots.

Those with experience and expertise know that Google has its uses but when it comes to ethical translations, the translator is like a tightrope walker, balancing deftly on the rope, after years of effort and practice and if he really needs to use the pole it is to aid his balance, not as a support in a simulation of stability. It would cause laughter and perhaps irritation if, instead of a daring show of acrobatics, his public found themselves watching the antics of a clown.

Translating means having complete proficiency in the functions of a language different to one's own, a perfect understanding of the cultural nuances and the structure of the text, in its semantic, syntactic, stylistic, phono symbolic, symbolic and "emotional" properties, and rendering its same meaning in one's native language.

I hope I've been a good tightrope walker and that, most of all, I have effectively transferred my emotions.

Soundtrack

The Yellow Rose

1) O' cafè - Roberto Murolo ed Enzo Gragnaniello

2) Rocco Hunt - Nu juorno buono

The Red Rose: the diary of my imperfections

3) Crawling - Linkin Park

4) Vasco Rossi - Gli Spari Sopra

Rose Rose -The Romance Scam

5) Roberto Vecchioni - Voglio una donna

6) Rkomi - Partire da te

Your notes:

Your notes:

Your notes:

Your notes:

Your notes:

Your notes:

Your notes:

Contents:

Introduction by Annalaura Confuorto	9
Author's Note	11
1. The Yellow Rose	17
2. The Red Rose - The Diary of my Imperfections	30
3. Rose Rose - The Romance Scam	48
About the Author	62
Afterword	64
Soundtrack	66
Your Notes	67

Printed by Amazon Italia Logistica S.r.l.
Torrazza Piemonte (TO), Italy

38557241R00047